To gassy folks everywhere.

—S.P.

Fart Squad
Text copyright © 2015 by Full Fathom Five, LLC
Illustrations copyright © 2015 by Full Fathom Five, LLC

Library of Congress Cataloging-in-Publication Data
Pilger, Seamus.
  Fart Squad / by Seamus Pilger. — First edition.
    pages cm — (Fart squad ; 1)
  Summary: After their lunches are stolen, Harry Buttz Elementary School students Darren, Tina,
Juan-Carlos, and Walter eat radioactive burritos that give each a strange ability—along with serious
gas—which, with training by Janitor Stan, may help them foil Number Two and the BO twins' evil plan.
  ISBN 978-0-06-236631-3 (hardback) — ISBN 978-0-06-229045-8 (pbk.)
  [1. Flatulence—Fiction. 2. Ability—Fiction. 3. Middle schools—Fiction. 4. Schools—Fiction. 5. Janitors—
Fiction. 6. Humorous stories.] I. Title.
PZ7.1.P55Far 2015   2014027412
[Fic]—dc23   CIP
                                                                                                            AC

Design by Victor Joseph Ochoa
15 16 17 18 19 CG/RRDH 10 9 8 7 6 5 4 3 2 1
❖
First Edition

FART SQUAD

by **SEAMUS PILGER**
illustrated by **STEPHEN GILPIN**

HARPER
An Imprint of HarperCollins*Publishers*

ahead of their class. A thick pair of glasses bounced atop his nose. He was smaller and skinnier than Darren even though he was only two days younger than his best friend. "Your lunch isn't going anywhere!"

"Except my stomach!" Darren said. He'd worked up an appetite in gym class and couldn't wait to get back to their classroom, where their lunches were stashed on a shelf in the coat closet. "I'm starving. Stuck-in-the-desert, eat-your-own-leg starving!"

Darren expected that he and Andy would be the first ones back to the classroom, so he was surprised to find two kids, Bertha and Oscar Scroggy, rummaging around in the coat closet—where they didn't belong.

Bertha and Oscar were brother and sister. Everyone called them B.O.—in part because they were inseparable and in part because they were allergic to bathing. Darren recognized their smell before he even saw their faces.

"Hey!" he challenged them. "What are you doing here?"

The twins wheeled about as though surprised by the interruption. "None of your business, squirt," Bertha said with her mouth full. "Get lost."

"Yeah," Oscar snarled. "What she said."

The twins were the biggest bullies in school, in more ways than one. They had been held back so many times they were practically teenagers, and they weren't above using their size advantage to terrorize everybody else. Most kids tried to stay out of their way.

But Darren didn't back down. "This is our classroom, not yours."

Andy looked at Darren like he was crazy, but stood by his friend. "Um, maybe you took a wrong turn?"

"Oh, yeah?" Bertha said, ignoring Andy. She and Oscar stomped toward the boys, clenching their fists. "You got a problem with that?"

Darren realized he might have rushed into things a little too fast . . . again. He felt bad about dragging Andy into this mess as well. One of these days he really needed to learn to control himself. . . .

He braced for some serious wedgy action—or worse—but was saved by the sound of the rest of their class catching up to them.

Bertha and Oscar scowled at the interruption. "Ah, this place is for babies anyway," Bertha muttered. She shoved her way past Darren and Andy and headed out into the hall. "C'mon, bro. We've got better places to be."

Oscar followed her out the door. "Later, losers."

Andy let out a sigh of relief. "Whew, that was a close one. What do you think they were doing here in the first place?"

"Nothing good," Darren guessed, but he was too hungry to worry about that now. His stomach was growling so loudly he could barely hear his own thoughts. He hurried over to the coatroom—but all that was there for him was a horrible discovery. "My lunch! It's missing!"

"Are you sure?" Andy helped him search the closet, even as the other kids arrived to claim their own lunch boxes and bag lunches. "Maybe you just misplaced it?"

"No!" Darren insisted. "I put it in the same place every day, right here on the shelf. You know I don't fool around when it comes to my lunch, especially on a day like today—pickles-and-sauerkraut sandwich—my favorite."

"The B.O. twins must have swiped it," Andy guessed. "Bertha had her mouth full, after all, and Oscar's pockets were bulging."

"I wouldn't put it past them," Darren said, but he was too hungry to worry about that now. "Must . . . have . . . food," he grunted. His legs felt like overcooked spaghetti, and his brain was foggy. "Get me to the cafeteria."

The hike to the cafeteria felt a zillion miles long. By the time they got there, most of their friends were already eating. Darren scrounged up some leftovers: an apple slice that was already turning brown, a pizza crust with teeth marks around the edge, and crumbs from the bottom of a crumpled bag of potato chips.

It wasn't enough. His body needed to refuel, and there was only one thing left to do.

"I'm gonna have to buy lunch."

Horrified gasps erupted around the table.

"You can't be serious!" Andy said. "Everybody knows that cafeteria food is roadkill."

"But I'm starving!" Darren insisted as he licked the last crumbs out of the bag of chips. "I've got no choice."

"Don't do it, man!" Andy pleaded. "Zero food is better than lunch-lady food!"

"I don't have a choice!" Darren said. He picked

up a tray and headed for the counter. "Wish me luck. I'm going in!"

Andy shook his head. "He's a dead man."

"Who? Darren?" Bootsie Brown arrived on the scene, sticking her nose in. Bootsie was the biggest snoop in school. She could smell another kid in trouble from two classrooms away. Her eyes zeroed in on Darren. "Okay, this I have to see!"

His friend's warnings rang in his ears as Darren got in the lunch line. To his horror, by the time he got his tray, all that was left was the infamous Five-Bean Burritos, the most dreaded of all the school lunches. A few of the specials, like the spaghetti or meat loaf, were at least semi-edible, but nobody in their right mind ever ate the burritos. Terrifying tales were told of what had happened to the last poor soul who had eaten them.

He eyed the burritos nervously. They looked as greasy and unappetizing as ever. Maybe even a little more so. But what could he do? Darren had run out of options. The horror stories had to just be rumors. How bad could they really be?

He piled a stack of greasy burri- tos onto his tray and carried them back to the table. A crowd of kids, including the B.O. twins, gath- ered around to watch.

"Bet you some nerd's lunch money that he throws up," Bertha said.

"You're on, sis," Oscar said, chortling. His breath smelled sus- piciously of pickles and sauerkraut, but Darren had more immediate concerns at the moment.

More kids joined the bet. The smart money was on some serious puking ... or worse.

"You know, the last kid who ate those had the runs for a month," Bootsie said. "It's true. I heard it from my cousin, who heard about it from a kid who knew a kid who used to go to this school...."

"Nah," Andy insisted. "I heard that a kid barfed so much that they had to bring in fire hoses to clean up the cafeteria afterward!"

Darren turned and gave the B.O. twins a dirty look. If anything like that went wrong, he'd have them to blame.

"Here goes nothing," he said.

The crowd gasped in amazement as he wolfed down the burritos in record time. They were crunchier than he had expected, with an odd flavor he couldn't place. So he doused them with Tabasco sauce and cleaned off his whole plate. There was absolutely no puking involved. Lunch money exchanged hands.

"I don't believe it," Bootsie said.

"Me either," Andy said. "You must have been *really* hungry!"

Darren spotted a few other worried-looking kids daring to eat today's "special." He wondered if their lunches had gone missing, too. He was gobbling down the last burrito when the bell rang. He patted his stomach, feeling full at last.

But then on the way back to his homeroom, he felt an uncomfortable pressure start to build. By the time he was back at his desk, an embarrassing eruption seemed inevitable. Half-digested burritos churned angrily, filling his gut with toxic gas. He clenched his butt to hold it in, but the pressure kept building.

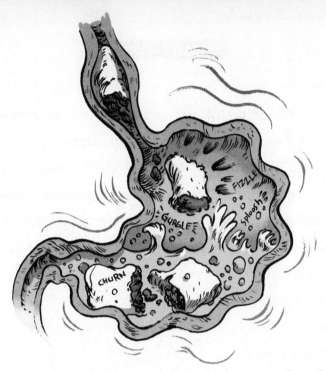

This was bad. Darren squirmed uncomfortably, hoping nobody would notice.

Fat chance.

"What's wrong with you?" Bootsie asked, loud enough for everyone to hear. Her hand shot up. "Miss Priscilly, Miss Priscilly, I think something's wrong with Dar—"

Darren gave her the evil eye.

The teacher, Miss Priscilly, glanced at him. "Are you all right, Darren?"

Miss Priscilly wasn't bad as teachers went, but she had one notable pet peeve. The young ladies and gentlemen of her classroom were expected to take control of their bodily functions or face the consequences. Mistakes were generally not allowed. Not long ago, a fellow classmate made the mistake of sneezing into his palm rather than into the crook of his elbow and wound up in the principal's office every recess for a week. Darren could only imagine where a burrito blooper from below the belt would land someone—especially if that someone was him.

"Uh-huh," he fibbed, barely able to sit still. He was clenching hard enough to turn coal into diamonds, but the volcanic eruption kept building inside him. His bloated stomach felt like it was about to burst. A chewed-up mess of burritos, Tabasco sauce, and soda boiled and bubbled in his belly. He knew he

SPLOOSH RUMBLE GURGLE

CLENCH

couldn't hold the fart in much longer.

Bootsie watched him like a hawk. Her nose twitched, anticipating trouble.

Darren had to think quickly or he was a goner. He was way past the point of asking for a bathroom pass. There was no telling what could happen on the long walk from his desk to the classroom door.

Then he had an idea.

Why not try to redirect the fart? Burps were rude, too, but probably not as smelly and embarrassing as a fart. He placed a hand over his mouth and tried to swallow backward.

But the burp came out louder than he expected. Heads turned in his direction.

"Miss Priscilly!" Bootsie piped up again.

That was hardly necessary.

"Darren!" the offended teacher said. "Kindly control yourself."

"I'm trying," he insisted, "but—"

A few desks away, Andy groaned and buried his face in his hands.

"Try harder," Miss Priscilly said sternly.

But the pressure was already building up inside Darren again—and heading down below this time. Before Darren could even try to burp again, he let loose with a fart that caught the entire classroom by surprise.

To be clear, this wasn't just any fart. This was the Fart to End All Farts. A *blatt* so rude the map of the world crashed to the floor. The explosive force

of the fart knocked Darren right out of his chair and landed him on the floor at the front of the class.

The fart was loud and gross. A sulfurous stink, strong enough to make your eyes water, filled the whole classroom. Students gagged and covered their mouths and noses. Others tried to hold their breaths. Bootsie pinched her nose shut and looked at Darren in complete disgust. Darren scrambled back to his seat—and found it hot to the touch. His eyes bulged as he saw that the plastic seat had *melted.* And Miss Priscilly was so furious her face turned ten shades of crimson.

"Oooooooooooooooooout!" she ordered.

"But—" He tried to explain that it wasn't his fault, really. "The burritos—"

"Mr. Stonkadopolis, what you eat is your business, as long as I don't have to see it, smell it, or think about it. But now you've made it my business, and the principal's business as well."

"I swear, it wasn't on purpose . . . !"

"Fine. Then go see the nurse . . . and don't come back without a note confirming that your digestive difficulties are under control," she said. "Quickly. Before you go off again!"

Darren hurried out of the classroom, his butt burning. So much for staying out of trouble!

And the worst part was, he felt an even bigger fart coming on. . . .

CHAPTER TWO

"I've told you before," the janitor said, "stay out of the basement."

As Darren trudged toward the nurse's office,  clutching his bloated stomach, he spotted a disturbance in the hall. Janitor Stan, who had been cleaning up at the school for as long as anyone could remember, was escorting Harry Buttz II and the B.O. twins out the basement door.

"You can't talk to me like that," Harry protested. "Don't you know who I am?"

Harry was the grandson of the school's namesake, a wealthy factory owner whose family had founded Buttzville generations ago. He had an expensive haircut, designer clothes, and, as usual, a hand down the back of his pants, furiously scratching at an itch that never seemed to go away, no matter what he tried. Despite his family name and all the campaign goodies he'd given away, he'd lost the last student body election because nobody would shake his hand.

"You tell him, Number Two!" Bertha said. She and Oscar hung out with Harry, mostly because he was rich and had all the newest computer games.

"Don't call me that!" Harry barked.

"Look, you three," Stan said. "I don't care what a big cheese Harry's dad is. The basement is off-limits.

Don't let me catch you snooping around there again."

"This is all your fault," Harry muttered to B.O. as the scratchy, smelly trio slunk away. "If you two could just follow simple directions . . ."

"Don't blame us," Bertha protested. "It's not our fault we were interrupted by a couple of nosy brats."

She glanced back over her shoulder, giving Darren the evil eye. Her hulking twin did likewise.

First the lunches, now this, Darren thought. *Those three are certainly keeping busy today.*

But before he could follow that thought through, he let another one rip. A thunderous fart echoed down the hall and polluted the air. There was no way Stan could miss it.

"Whoa!" the janitor exclaimed. "What was that?"

"Just some bad burritos," Darren explained.

"The lunchroom special?" Stan guessed. "Let me guess, Miss Priscilly sent you to the nurse's office, right?"

Nothing got past the eagle-eyed janitor, who always knew more about what was happening at the school than the principal and teachers. He knew which kids were friends, why certain kids weren't speaking to one another, what had become of any "misplaced" school supplies, and who exactly had toilet-papered the principal's car that one time. He had also covered for Darren in the past, like when all the biology class frogs had somehow gotten loose. (It was an accident. Really!)

"Something like that," Darren admitted. He tried to change the subject. "What was all that with Number Two and his goon squad?"

"No big deal," Stan said. "Just caught them poking around where they didn't belong . . . again. But don't let me slow you down. Run along now," he said, batting away the contaminated air in front of him. "Go see what the nurse can do for that unruly gut of yours."

Darren knew the way to the infirmary by heart, thanks to the many scrapes and sprains he had picked up playing too hard. When he got there, he found Nurse Rancid occupied with another patient: a tiny dark-haired girl in a pretty pink dress. She looked like a little princess. All that was missing was the tiara.

"Excuse me," he said. "Miss Priscilly sent me...."

"Just take a seat," the nurse replied. "I'll be with you in a sec."

But before Darren sat down, a foul smell filled the office. It was strong enough to make Darren hold his nose, but the effect on Nurse Rancid was even more impressive. "Oh my!" she gasped before collapsing onto the floor. She was out cold. This was not good. Darren needed a note from her if he wanted to get back to class, but as long as Nurse Rancid was passed out she wasn't going to be doing any writing of any kind.

Yikes, Darren thought. *Did I do that?*

He was pretty sure he hadn't farted this time, which left only one other suspect.

"Did *you* do that?" he asked the girl.

"Do what?" she asked innocently.

Darren furiously fanned Nurse Rancid in the hopes of reviving her. "You know...," he said. "Fart."

"Did you hear a fart?" she asked.

"No," he admitted.

"Then I must not have," she said.

"Or maybe your farts are just silent but deadly."

Just then, Nurse Rancid stirred. Darren ran to her desk to get a pen and notepad before she passed out again. Sure the nurse hadn't yet examined him, but maybe she'd be out of it enough not to realize. Because all he really needed to satisfy Miss Priscilly was a signed note.

But as soon as the nurse opened her eyes, an awful, pungent smell flooded the room and knocked her out cold again.

This time Darren *knew* he wasn't responsible. It had to be the girl again.

"Knock that off!" he said sharply.

"Knock what off?" she replied.

"You know what I mean!"

To be fair, holding a fart in was easier said than done. Before Darren could say another word, he lost control himself. A titanic *blatt*, twice as loud and hot as before, scorched the seat of his favorite jeans.

Okay, he thought. *That one was me.*

"Excuse me," the girl said politely. "It seems your butt is smoking."

Darren grimaced in pain. The fart didn't just smell. It burned!

"Hang on!" The girl strolled over to the infirmary's small fridge and grabbed a handful of colored medicinal Popsicles. "Maybe these will help!"

Couldn't hurt, Darren thought. He grabbed the Popsicles, ripped off the wrappers, and jammed them down the seat of his pants. Steam rose from his backside. He was a sticky mess, but at least his butt wasn't on fire anymore.

"You're welcome," the girl said. "My name's Tina, by the way. Tina Heiney."

"Darren," he introduced himself. "And thanks."

Two more kids entered the office, clutching their stomachs.

"Say, do I detect the enticing aroma of Popsicles?" Walter Turnip asked. Darren recognized him from another fourth-grade class. As tall as he was wide, Walter was hard to miss. But today his bulging belly appeared even bigger than usual, like an overinflated balloon. He looked like a blimp in a rumpled T-shirt. And unless Darren was imagin-

ing things, Walter appeared to be floating a few inches off the floor, at least until a noisy fart released some gas and he touched down again. "Never mind. My digestive tract feels a trifle unsettled."

As always, Juan-Carlos Finkelstein was by Walter's side. He was tall, too, but in a lanky way. "I always said he was full of hot air, but this is taking it too far!"

Juan-C still needed a note for Miss Priscilly. number-ed toward the nurse with the notepad, but funny. I_he could even hand her the pen, a silent right no_f not-so-fresh air knocked her out again. Her gling _drooped forward onto her chest.
across_arren scowled at Tina.

loud a

been

san

ha

ti

c

c

lu

b

SHUDDER

Tina shrugged. "Sorry. It just slipped out."

"Pardon me, but that's simply not normal," Walter said.

"That's for sure," Juan-Carlos agreed.

Just then, Janitor Stan poked his head into the office and saw the nurse slumped on the floor. "Er, what's the matter with her?"

Darren wasn't quite ready to spill the beans, as it were.

"Beats me," he said. "Maybe she's been working too hard?"

The other kids did not contradict him. Who wanted to be known for having farts nasty enough to flatten the school nurse?

"I see," Stan said, sounding unconvinced. He looked the kids over and sniffed the air. "Why don't you kids come back another time? I think she just needs a break and a little fresh air. Or, to be more exact, *fresher* air."

Darren hesitated. "Er, I still need a note—or Miss Priscilly won't let me back into class."

Stan took the pad and scribbled a note, forging Nurse Rancid's name. He winked at Darren. "Nobody can read her handwriting anyway. Now scoot!"

Darren headed toward the door. He had his note, but he had plenty of questions, too. Something was in the air all right. He just wished he knew what it was.

What was in those burritos anyway?

CHAPTER THREE

It was recess, and the playground on the roof of the school was filled with kids enjoying the fresh air. Ordinarily Darren would be in the thick of things, trying to burn off all his excess energy, but today he kept to the sidelines, avoiding everybody but Andy. His stomach was still churning, and he was clenching hard against another gas eruption.

"Boy, those burritos really did a number on you," Andy said sympathetically. "You think you can get through class without farting again?"

"I hope so," Darren said uncertainly.

He spotted Harry Buttz and the B.O. twins hanging out together across the yard, shunned by everybody else. This was all their fault, Darren realized. If B.O. hadn't swiped his lunch, he wouldn't have had to eat those darn burritos! He wouldn't have farted in class. And he would be dreaming about sports camp instead of worrying about summer school.

His temper took over, and he stormed across the roof to confront the bullies.

"Wait!" Andy called out, but once Darren got going there was no slowing him down. "Great," Andy muttered. "Here we go again. . . ."

As Darren got closer to the threesome, he could hear Harry giving his flunkies a hard time. "You're going to have to do better next time," he scolded. "Four lost lunches wasn't nearly enough to—"

"I knew it!" Darren said, butting in, as Andy ran to keep up. Darren could only guess what Harry meant by "next time," but the part about the "lost lunches" only confirmed his suspicions.

"You people are nothing but a rotten bunch of lunch thieves!"

"Beat it, Stonkadopolis," Harry said. "Mind

your own business."

"Hey!" Bertha said, recognizing Darren and Andy. "These are the dweebs who interrupted us before."

"Yeah," Oscar confirmed. "They're the ones who spoiled things, so we couldn't—"

"Shut your trap," Harry barked, as though Oscar was about to say too much. He scowled at Darren and Andy. "Are you two deaf? Get lost."

Harry's reaction convinced Darren that the stolen lunches were part of some larger plot.

"What's this all about?" he demanded. "Does it

have something to do with you snooping around the basement?"

"Basement?" Andy asked, completely lost.

Harry's scowl turned into a glare. "If you were smart, you'd stop being so nosy." He nodded at B.O. "Show these punks what happens to people who ask too many questions."

"You bet, Number Two," Bertha said.

"Don't call me that!"

"Sorry," Oscar said on his sister's behalf.

The twins closed in on Darren and Andy while Harry hung back, content to let B.O. do the dirty work. Darren gulped, realizing that he really hadn't thought this through. He glanced around, but didn't see any teachers watching. Not that it mattered. Thanks to his family connections, Harry got away with a lot at Harry Buttz Elementary.

"You two got lucky before," Bertha said, "but not this time."

Oscar cracked his knuckles. "'Bout time you got what's coming to you."

"Hang on!" Andy took off his glasses and looked around for a safe place to put them. "I don't think I want to see this anyway."

Darren figured they were goners, unless . . .

He spun around and let loose with a volcanic fart that blasted the twins off their feet. They tumbled backward, gasping and choking at the stench. Their eyebrows were singed from the heat of the

eruption. A few feet back, Harry's jaw dropped and his eyes widened.

"The burritos," he realized. "They must be even gassier than anyone thought possible!"

Darren grabbed Andy by the arm and dragged him away.

"Later, losers!" he said as Andy put his glasses back on. He looked around in confusion. "What happened?"

Darren just grinned.

Maybe there *were* advantages to having the hottest farts in school.

CHAPTER FOUR

Darren still needed to get back in Miss Priscilly's good graces, or kiss sports camp good-bye. "Is there any way I can earn some extra credit?" he asked.

"The town's one-hundredth birthday is coming up," the teacher said. "So why don't you write up a report on the history of Buttzville?"

Darren knew he had to get an *A* on the report. At this point, he needed all the extra credit he could get to stay out of summer school. During study hall, he and Andy headed straight for the school library. Darren was grateful for his friend's help. Andy got much better grades than Darren did, probably because he could actually sit still and study sometimes!

They took every book on the history of Buttz-ville off the shelf. Most of them were covered with dust, no doubt because no one ever read any of them. But there was one that seemed less dusty than the others: *The Buttz Family Chronicles.*

Andy cracked it open and started reading. Darren peered over his shoulder.

Herein lies a true account of the Family Buttz, the book began, *and the terrible curse that hath long afflicted them. . . .*

"Curse?" Darren said. "That sounds interesting."

"I'll say," Andy agreed. "Listen to this. . . ."

According to the book, the Buttzes had always been cursed with a never-ending butt itch. The curse had been passed down from generation to generation, all the way back to the old country. The Buttzes were doomed to scratch themselves forever until one of Harry's ancestors, an alchemist named Scabious Buttz, found a cure for their condition by—

The rest of the pages about the curse had been ripped out. When the book picked up again, the Buttzes were busily founding the town and making their fortune. Nothing more was written about the curse.

"What the—" Darren objected. "Where's the rest of it?"

"Gone," Andy said.

Darren was puzzled. If Scabious had found a

cure, why was Harry Buttz still scratching? Darren couldn't help wondering if this had something to do with why B.O. had stolen those sandwiches—and whatever it was Harry was up to "next time."

Darren checked to see if there was another copy of the book on the shelves, but no such luck. Frustrated, he went up to the librarian's desk. "Excuse me," he asked. "Can you tell me who checked out this book last? It appears to be damaged."

The librarian checked her records. "Harry Buttz the Second checked it out just a few weeks ago."

"Is that so?" Darren said. "I should have known."

Now Darren had to find out what was on the missing pages.

But how?

CHAPTER FIVE

The next day found Darren stuck at a school assembly and not very happy about it. He was not a big fan of school assemblies. It was too much sitting around on the bleachers in the gym, and the Harry Buttz Elementary School gym almost smelled worse than farts. It stank of chlorine so bad it made Darren's eyes water. Some genius had had the brilliant idea to build a retractable floor and put the school pool right underneath it. Assemblies were the worst. And this one was the worst of the worst—a boring presentation on the history of the town, complete with a slide show and speeches!

"Generations ago, this was just worthless

swampland," Principal Dingleberry said into a microphone down on the floor of the gym. "But from the stagnant depths of a polluted marsh rose Harry Buttz Elementary School. Mr. Buttz could

not be with us today, but his illustrious family is represented by our own Harry Buttz, or, as his friends call him, 'Number Two'!"

Harry gave the principal a dirty look. She knew how much he hated to be called that. He stood beside her, squirming awkwardly, hands tucked deeply into his pants pockets.

"Bet you a week's allowance," Darren whispered to Andy,

"that Harry can't get through this assembly without scratching his butt."

"Forget it," Andy said. "I'm not dumb enough to take that bet."

Sure enough, within moments Harry was reaching around and scratching himself onstage. Snickers and giggles rippled through the audience.

"And there he goes . . . ," Andy said, grinning.

"Just like in that history book," Darren whispered, remembering what they'd read about the Buttz family curse. "I still wish I knew what those missing pages said. . . . For my report, of course."

"You know, I've been thinking about that," Andy said. "We might be able to find the answer on the Internet. If you want, we can search for it this weekend." He paused to sniff the air. "Hey, who farted?"

"Don't look at me," Darren insisted. His stomach was still rumbling like a restless volcano, but he didn't *think* that fart came from him. Glancing around, he spotted Walter Turnip sitting a few rows behind them in the bleachers. Looking rounder than ever, Walter was holding onto the bench with both hands to keep from lifting off into the air!

Uh-oh, Darren thought.

He scanned the gym until he located Tina and Juan-Carlos, who had also noticed Walter's predicament. This wasn't good. If Walter got caught floating around, the whole school— heck, maybe even the whole world— would find out just how freaky their farts had become. They exchanged looks, realizing that something had to be done. Just the fear of being exposed as an uncontrollable explosive farter agitated Darren's stomach. He guessed that the others were having the same reaction. They had to clear the gym before Walter floated away.

Darren had an idea, but it was going to take teamwork.

He took out his phone and furtively texted the others:

ON THE COUNT OF THREE . . .

The farty foursome nodded at one another.

"One . . ." Darren mouthed, raising his index finger. "Two . . ." then his middle finger. "Three . . ." and his ring finger. . . .

And then they all let one rip simultaneously.

Suddenly, the entire gym reeked like the world's biggest fart. The disgusting odor was everywhere, making it impossible to tell where the fart had come from. Gagging and holding their noses, everyone dashed for the exits.

CLICKITY CLICKY CLICKITY

"This assembly is over!" the principal shouted. "Please exit in an orderly fashion!" Then she dropped her microphone and ran screaming out of the gym.

Andy was halfway to the door before he noticed that Darren wasn't following him.

"What are you waiting for?" he called. "We gotta get out of here. This place stinks, big time!"

"Don't worry about me!" Darren shouted. "I'm right behind you!"

He felt bad about lying to his best friend, but this wasn't his secret to share.

The gasping crowd carried Andy away, and

within minutes the gym was deserted except for Darren and his flatulent accomplices.

And just in time!

Superinflated, Walter lost his grip on the bleachers and shot up toward the ceiling. Random farts sent him jetting about in the air like a leaky balloon. High above the floor, he bounced off the walls and ceiling.

"Your assistance, please!" he hollered. "I can't get down!"

Darren and the others stared up at him, unsure what to do.

"Do we try to lasso him?" Juan-Carlos asked.

"I don't think I can throw that high," Darren said. "Maybe he'll run out of gas?"

Walter doubted it. "Not the way my stomach is still churning."

"Ditto," Tina confirmed.

"And all this excitement is just making it worse!"

Then, as if things weren't bad enough, Bootsie barged back into the gym, snooping as usual. "Hey! What's going on in here?"

"Er, nothing," Darren said. "Why do you ask?"

Bootsie looked around suspiciously. She hadn't spotted Walter overhead yet, but it was only a matter of time. Her nose twitched, sniffing for trouble.

"I heard somebody shouting," she insisted.

Tina came up beside her. Bootsie's nose twitched again—and she passed out on the floor.

"Bet you didn't hear that," Tina said, smirking.

"Thanks!" Darren said. He dragged Bootsie out of the way. "But we still need to get Walter down before anybody else shows up." He shouted up at the floating kid. "Try to propel yourself by pointing your butt at the ceiling!"

"But I'll crash and crack my head open," Walter yelped.

"Not if we open the pool!" Darren said. There was a full-sized swimming pool under the floor of the gym. The floors just needed to be retracted. "Juan-Carlos! Find the controls!"

"Already on it!" Juan-Carlos said. "Time for a water landing!"

A sign above the controls read DO NOT TOUCH! Juan-Carlos ignored it.

He flicked the switch. Hidden motors hummed as the gym floor split down the middle,

revealing the bright blue waters of the pool.

"C'mon, Walter!" Darren shouted. "You can do it! Just point your butt in the right direction!"

Walter rolled in the air, high above them. He tried to orient himself.

"Very well," he said nervously. "Wish me luck!"

Then a supersonic fart sent him rocketing down toward the pool.

Splashdown!

POOT

A huge wave soaked Darren, Juan-Carlos, and Tina, but they hurried to fish Walter from the pool regardless. Dripping wet, he was even heavier than he looked.

"Wow!" Juan-Carlos said. "That was a real power dive! You practically emptied the pool!"

Walter looked like he was just glad to be on solid ground again.

Darren's sneakers sloshed. The gym was flooded. They were so going to be busted.

"I'll handle this mess," Stan the janitor said. He appeared as if from nowhere, mop in hand. He winked at the kids. "You better make tracks before you end up having to answer some very awkward questions."

"Thanks, Stan," Darren said. "But—"

"Meet me by the janitor's closet," Stan said. "All of you."

Darren hesitated, wanting answers, but Tina tugged on his arm. "You heard the man. Let's go— unless you want everybody to know your butt is a biohazard!"

"Good point," Darren said, heading for the nearest exit as he wondered what in the world Stan could possibly want to talk about.

CHAPTER SIX

"**I** thought I smelled you coming!" Stan said.

Darren and his new friends crowded into the janitor's closet, which was stuffed with mops, brooms, and buckets.

"Sorry about the smell . . . ," Darren said. "It's like these farts are supercharged or something!"

"Is that so?" Stan seemed very interested in what Darren had to say. "Tell me more."

Darren explained how each kid's farts worked. It was such a relief to be able to talk about the farts  to *someone* outside the foursome. Walter could blast off into the air.

Juan-Carlos's farts were time bombs, going off minutes after he'd planted them.

 Tina's were stealth bombs that made no noise but stank worse than a sewer explosion. And Darren's burned like fire.

"There's nothing natural about these farts," Darren insisted.

"It's the burritos," Stan explained. "The lunch lady doesn't like to waste any food. So ever since the burritos got their bad rap and kids stopped eating them, she's taken to throwing the leftovers in the microwave every day. At this point, they've been heated and reheated so many times they're undoubtedly radioactive. I wouldn't be surprised if they glowed in the dark!"

"So mutated beans turned us into mutant beings?" Juan-Carlos joked.

"Something like that," Stan said.

"And you know this how?" Tina asked.

"Just by keeping my eyes open," the janitor said. "Trust me, I take out the trash every day, and the lunchroom has *never* tossed out any uneaten burritos."

"But nobody ever eats them," Juan-Carlos said. "Unless they have to."

"We did," Tina said. "Because the B.O. twins swiped our lunches."

"Wait a second," Darren said. "What if the B.O. twins swiped our lunches because they wanted us to eat those toxic burritos?"

"Actually, they weren't all that unappetizing," Walter said. His bulging stomach grumbled. "Is it lunchtime yet?"

"Don't even think about it," Tina said. "We're not peeling you off the ceiling again."

Juan-Carlos was still confused. "But what was the point? Why would they want to force people to eat bad burritos?"

"I'm not sure," Darren admitted. He felt like a puzzle was coming together, but he didn't have all the pieces yet. "But I'm pretty sure it was Harry Buttz's idea . . . and that he's not done yet."

Tina raised her hand. "If we don't eat the burritos again, will our farts go back to normal?"

"Possibly," Stan said, "but do you really want them to? Seems to me you've all been given some very special gifts. Smelly, but special." His voice grew more serious. "You know what they say:

FROM GREAT FARTS COME MIGHTY WINDS.

"Er, I don't think anybody actually says that," Juan-Carlos said.

"Think about the possibilities. The question is do you want to lose your new fart abilities . . . or learn to control them?"

Darren remembered how he had bowled over the B.O. twins with a well-timed fart, saving himself and Andy from the bullies. And how he and the others had used their powers to clear the auditorium and get Walter off the ceiling. Granted, without the new fart abilities Walter wouldn't have been anywhere near the ceiling to begin with, but still, their new "gifts" had opened up a lot of possibilities for them.

"Control them?" he asked. "How?"

"I can teach you," Stan volunteered, putting on a rising-sun headband. "I can be your 'scent-sei.'"

"Good one," said Juan-Carlos. "I wish I had come up with that."

Tina raised her hand again. "Sir, why you? No offense."

"I'm the janitor," he reminded her. "Smelly stuff is my specialty."

Juan-Carlos shrugged. "Makes sense to me."

"Listen," Stan urged them, "you've already proven that you make a great team. With a little coaching, you can become . . . the Fart Squad!"

"But we're not heroes," Darren said. "Why would we need superpowers? It's not like there are any real bad guys around."

Stan shook his head in disbelief. "Are you sure about that?"

Darren thought of Harry Buttz and B.O., who he was pretty sure were up to no good. There were the stolen lunches, after all, and the way Harry and the twins had tried to sneak into the school basement afterward. They were after something, but what? Did it have to do with the Buttz family curse—and the missing pages?

"I overheard Harry say something to B.O. about 'next time,'" he told the others. "I don't know exactly what he meant, but I don't think this is over yet . . . whatever it is."

"So maybe the Fart Squad needs to be ready," Stan said.

"For what?" Tina asked.

Darren wished he knew.

CHAPTER SEVEN

"**W**elcome to Fart Boot Camp!" Stan greeted them.

The janitor used his keys to let them into the school. Darren usually hung out with Andy on Saturdays. He felt bad about ditching his friend on a weekend, especially after Andy had volunteered to help Darren with his report, but Stan had sworn the entire "Fart Squad" to secrecy. According to him, the fewer people who knew about them, the better.

Stan had set up the gym to be a secret training center, with padded wrestling mats and even a trampoline in place. A tray of freshly microwaved burritos waited on top of a wheeled cart. Stan must

have raided the lunchroom freezer. Darren tried not to think about how old the burritos might be.

"Time to power up!" Stan said. "Dig in!"

Walter, Juan-Carlos, and Tina helped themselves to the greasy "fuel," but Darren held back. He was having second thoughts about this whole Fart Squad business. True, superfarts might come in handy from time to time. But now that his flaming farts were starting to cool off a little, he was reminded of how nice it feels to have a burn-free butt.

"Who wants to go first?" Stan asked.

Juan-Carlos volunteered. "Just watch me, boys and girl. I'm cookin' with gas!"

He paused, waiting for a laugh that failed to come.

"Gas, get it?" he asked.

"I'm sure they did, Juan-Carlos. You can work on your comedy later," Stan said. "Or not," he added under his breath. Stan marked an X on the floor with chalk. "Why don't you plant a stink bomb here ... and see if you can keep it from going off for a full ten seconds?"

"You bet," Juan-Carlos said, taking his place on the X. He concentrated hard, then hurried away before the stink bomb went off. Stan took out a stopwatch. He counted down the seconds.

"Ten, nine, eight, seven, six, five, four, three, two, one ..."

Nothing happened. Nobody heard or smelled anything nasty.

"You laid a dud, dude," Walter teased. "To use the vernacular."

"I farted, I swear," Juan-Carlos insisted. "Cross my heart . . . and my butt!"

Stan strolled over to the X to investigate—just as a stink bomb went off—five seconds late. He was knocked off his feet by force of the fart.

"Whew!" he said. "That was a ripe one!"

Darren and Walter helped Stan to his feet. He wiped the tears from his eyes.

"I think you need a little more practice," the janitor said. "Timing is everything, especially where farts are concerned!"

"Tell me about it," Juan-Carlos said, blushing.

Tina raised her hand. "Let me go next, please."

Juan-Carlos stepped aside. "Go for it, Tiny."

"*Tina,*" she corrected him. "Don't call me Tiny."

"I don't know," Juan-Carlos joked. "You look pretty tiny to—"

A silent fart knocked him out. He collapsed onto a mat.

Darren stared at the petite little princess. "That was an accident, right?"

"Totally," she said sweetly. "Sorry."

They all backed away from her, just to be safe. Stan had to dump a bucket of water over Juan-Carlos's head to wake him up.

Stan eyed Tina warily. She seemed so harmless, and yet . . .

"On second thought," he said, "maybe we should

give Walter some flight practice now."

Stan fitted Walter with a crash helmet and tied a safety rope around him so they could pull him back to earth if necessary. The rest of the squad helped push the trampoline to the center of the floor.

"All right," Stan declared. "You're prepped for takeoff. Fart, fart, and away!"

Walter polished off another burrito, then let loose with a jet of gas that lifted him off the floor. For a moment, it looked like he was going to slam headfirst into the ceiling, but he changed course at the last second. He zipped around overhead like a hot-air balloon gone berserk.

"Try to control your flight," Stan coached him. "Nice smooth circles!"

But Walter was spinning and looping and

zigzagging wildly above them. He grabbed frantically for a basketball hoop to anchor himself, but missed. Noisy farts propelled him every which way.

"Oh dear!" he shrieked. "I suspect I should not have indulged in that second burrito!"

Darren chased after the dangling safety rope. "Don't worry! We'll pull you down!"

He grabbed the rope, hoping to reel the flying kid in, but Walter's farts had more lift than he'd expected. Before he knew it, Darren took flight as well.

"Hang on, Darren!" Tina yelled. "Don't let go!"

She, Juan-Carlos, and Stan pushed the trampoline back and forth across the floor, trying to keep it under their airborne friends. Darren gulped when he looked down and saw how far up he was.

"Get us down!" he yelled at Walter. "This is crazy!"

"I'm endeavoring to do just that!" Walter yelled.

The extra weight began to drag Walter down. Darren pulled himself up the rope so that more of it dangled below him. Stan and the other kids grabbed the rope and pulled Darren and Walter toward the trampoline. Darren waited until it was directly beneath him, then let go of the line.

"AAAAAAA!" he screamed as he fell.

He hit the trampoline and bounced off it onto the floor. The mats cushioned his crash landing . . . a little. His poor butt was going to be black and blue, on top of being burnt.

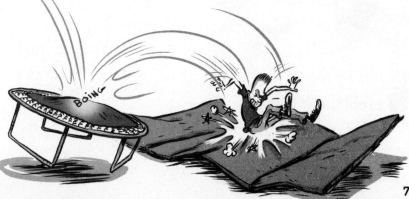

"Don't just sit there!" Tina called. "Help us get Walter down!"

Working together, Stan and the squad finally managed to tug Walter safely down. Juan-Carlos borrowed a barbell from the gym storeroom to weigh down Walter so that he wouldn't take off again.

"Don't be discouraged," Stan told Walter. "You just need more practice."

"Wonderful," Walter said glumly. "I can scarcely wait."

Now it was Darren's turn. Stan noticed that Darren hadn't tried the burritos yet.

"What's the matter, Darren?" the janitor asked gently. "Is there a problem?"

"I'm not sure about this," Darren confessed.

"You don't realize how hot my farts get."

"I'm not surprised," Stan said. "You've always had plenty of energy to burn. But the Fart Squad needs you, Darren. You're a born leader. I can tell. Just look at how you rushed to help Walter earlier."

Darren appreciated the pep talk, but he was still uneasy. "But what if my farts are too hot to handle?"

"All the more reason to find out just how scorching they can get," Stan said. He wheeled the cart of burritos toward Darren. "These have gone cold. Let's see if you can reheat them."

"Um, we're not going to have to eat them afterward, are we?" Juan-Carlos asked. "'Cause I think I'm allergic to fart-cooked food."

"Don't worry," Stan said. "There are plenty more where these came from." He stuck a cooking thermometer into the cold burritos. "Go ahead, Darren. Bake those beans."

Darren didn't want to let the others down. He forced down half a cold burrito and turned his backside toward the rest. His stomach started gurgling right away. He felt the hot gas building inside his gut.

"Watch out!" he warned. "Fire in the hole!"

A volcanic fart erupted through the seat of his jeans. He tried to control it, but it was like a blowtorch. The thermometer blew its top. Overheated burritos exploded, spraying beans everywhere. Goopy burrito guts were splattered over everyone's hair and clothes. Even Tina was a mess.

"Noooooooooooooooooo!" she exclaimed in horror. "I've been burrito'd!"

"I'm sorry!" Darren shouted. "I told you I couldn't control it!"

Darren surveyed the damage. Thanks to him, his new friends looked like they had just gone swimming in vomit, there was a gaping hole in his pants, and he'd made a giant fool out of himself.

Not exactly the picture of a future leader.

CHAPTER EIGHT

"**S**o where were you on Saturday?" Andy asked. "I thought I was going to help you with your report?"

"Um, my folks grounded me," Darren fibbed. It was recess, and they were catching up in the school yard. Darren felt bad about lying to his friend, but what else could he do? "Thanks for offering, though."

"Get ready to thank me some more," Andy said, bubbling over with excitement. "Guess what? I found the missing pages from that old book on the Buttz family!"

Darren couldn't believe his ears. "Really?"

"Yep!" Andy couldn't wait to fill him in. "I searched around online and finally found some scans of another copy of the book." He pulled the printouts from his backpack. "It's all here— everything about the curse and the cure and what happened next."

Darren was too impatient to read through the pages. "Tell me!"

"Okay," Andy said. "As you know, legend has it

that the Buttzes' never-ending itch goes way, way back. But generations ago, Harry's great-great-not-sure-how-many-greats grandfather, Scabious Buttz, forged the Golden Scratcher, a magical golden butt scratcher that brought them some relief. The catch? There's only so much itchiness the Scratcher can handle before it gets overloaded, like a dam that's holding back too much water. At a certain point, people got worried that the Scratcher was on the verge of spilling all that concentrated itchiness all over Buttzville, so concerned citizens stole the Scratcher and buried it in a swamp where they were sure nobody would ever find it. But guess where the town eventually built the new elementary school?"

"Right on top of the Scratcher," Darren realized.

"Bingo," Andy said. "At least according to the legend, that is."

That's what Harry is looking for in the basement, Darren realized, putting more of the pieces of the puzzle together. Harry was determined to cure his itchy behind, no matter the risk to the town. But where did the bad burritos and stolen lunches fit in? Darren felt like he was still missing something.

The lunch bell rang and they headed inside, only to find a crowd of hungry kids tugging at the door to the coatroom. Miss Priscilly stood by helplessly, looking overwhelmed.

"What is it?" Darren asked, his stomach grumbling. "What's the matter?"

"Somebody superglued the lock shut," Bootsie said, eager to be the bearer of bad news. "Nobody can get to their lunch boxes!"

"That sucks," Andy said to Darren. "Looks like we're all going to have to try the lunchroom special today."

Darren's jaw dropped. "Oh my gosh," he exclaimed.

Suddenly, it all made sense, sorta. This was what Harry had wanted to do all along, to get the entire school so farty, they'd be forced to evacuate the building, so that he could get to the basement and dig up the Golden Scratcher.

"Uh-oh," Darren gasped. "This isn't good."

The very idea of Harry getting his hands on the Scratcher made Darren's stomach churn. Harry's itchy butt might be enough to push the Scratcher

over the edge and to flood the entire town with never-ending itches!

Darren thought about melting the glue with a volcanic fart, but after what happened with the beans, that didn't seem like a good idea. Even if he didn't scorch all the lunches by accident, who would want to eat food that had been farted on?

Plus, he couldn't exactly unleash a fart in front of Miss Priscilly....

He had to find *another* way to stop anybody else from eating those burritos!

"I just remembered there's something I have to do," Darren told Andy. He dashed toward the cafeteria. "Gotta run!"

Darren hated ditching Andy again, but there was no time to lose. He raced into the cafeteria at top speed.

Sure enough, there were already plenty of students lined up for today's lunch: "Magic Monday Burritos." Darren shuddered at the thought of all those kids consuming the radioactive beans. The four members of the Fart Squad were one thing, but hundreds of kids farting with complete abandon would be a catastrophe. The entire school would be one big gassy chain reaction. They would have to clear out the building—and give Harry a straight shot at the Golden Scratcher.

Unless Darren did something right away.

"Excuse me!" he shouted, cutting to the head of the line. "Comin' through!"

Angry voices protested his lack of proper lunch line etiquette, but Darren ignored them. Instead he grabbed the burritos off every kid's tray, before anyone else could eat one, and started wolfing them down with his bare hands. A familiar rumble ignited in his stomach.

Time to fight fire with fire, he thought. *Just one decent fart might be enough to empty the cafeteria—and kill everybody's appetite.*

"Whoa," he warned, clutching his stomach. "Better stay away from those burritos. I feel something nasty coming on!"

The fart erupted like a volcano, charring his pants. The line behind him broke apart as gagging students scrambled to get away from the sickening odor. For a moment, Darren thought he had saved the day. Nobody else was going to be eating those burritos now!

But then a second fart erupted from him. This one was even bigger and hotter than the first. It set off the fire alarm.

And the sprinkler system.

Cold water sprayed down from the ceiling. Shrieking kids ran from the cafeteria and out of the building. A blaring siren drove everybody toward the exits. Soaked, Darren spotted Janitor Stan assisting in the evacuation, along with all the other teachers and staff.

"Oh no!" Darren realized. His plan had back-fired . . . in more ways than one.

This was exactly the kind of distraction Harry had been trying to arrange!

Darren looked around, but didn't see Harry or the B.O. twins anywhere. Buttzville was in danger, Darren realized, and it was all his fault because he hadn't been able to control the superheated gas-ses surging inside him. He knew he had to make things right, even if it meant gobbling more radio-active burritos. He took out his phone and texted the rest of the Fart Squad:

BASEMENT—ASAP!

Ignoring the fire alarm, he filled a tray with burritos and sprinted to the basement entrance, his sneakers sloshing noisily. Walter, Juan-Carlos, and Tina came running to join him.

"What's up?" Juan-Carlos asked. "Where's the fire?" He waited for a laugh. "Fire, get it? 'Cause, you know, the alarm?"

SQUISH SPLOOSH SQUISHY

Darren ignored him. "It's Harry Buttz!" he said. "He's after the Golden Scratcher!"

"The golden what?" Tina asked.

Darren remembered that the other Squad members hadn't heard that part of the legend yet. He quickly filled them in even as he worried about

Harry getting to the Scratcher at last. Scabious Buttz's unnatural invention had been buried for a reason. . . .

"We need to keep that Scratcher away from Harry and his goons—before they accidentally unleash an avalanche of itchiness on the whole town!"

"Hold on there!" Walter said. "An enchanted butt scratcher? Really?"

"Says the guy who can float like a balloon," Juan-Carlos pointed out.

"Touché." Walter put on his crash helmet. "So what do we do now?"

"Just what Stan trained us to do," Darren said firmly, his mind made up. "The Fart Squad needs to go into action!" He realized now that the canny janitor had been right all along. "From great farts come mighty winds!"

He held out the tray of greasy burritos.

"Eat up!"

CHAPTER NINE

The Fart Squad refueled in a hurry. Tina and Juan-Carlos scarfed down a burrito each, while Walter somehow managed to polish off two in the same amount of time. "I must say," he said with his mouth full, "I'm developing a real taste for these succulent morsels."

"Just hurry up and swallow," Darren said. "Harry and B.O. could be digging up the Scratcher at this very moment!"

Tina emitted an oddly delicate burp. "I'm ready if you are."

"Me, too," Juan-Carlos said, patting his stomach. "Let's kick some Buttz!"

They raced down the stairs, taking the steps two at a time. Darren heard banging noises and cussing down below. They rushed into the basement in time to see Harry Buttz lifting a package from a freshly dug hole in the basement floor. The B.O. twins stood nearby, sweating heavily, which made them smell even worse. Bertha gripped a shovel with both hands. Oscar held a sledgehammer. And was that a jackhammer in the corner?

"Finally!" Harry exclaimed. "I found it!" He held up a battered wooden chest about a foot long. He fumbled with a rusty latch, trying to pry it open.

"Put that back where it belongs, Harry!" Darren shouted. "It's too dangerous to mess with!"

Harry was startled by the interruption. "You again, Stonkadopolis?" He spotted the rest of the Fart Squad as well. "And you brought friends?"

"We can't let you use the Scratcher," Darren said. "It's too dangerous!"

"Try and stop me," Harry said, sneering. He nodded at B.O. "Keep them away from me, and I'll buy you all the computer games you want!"

"No problem, Number Two," Bertha said.

"Don't call me that!"

"Sorry!"

She swung the shovel at Walter, who farted in alarm. A burst of hot air shot him up to the ceiling so that the shovel passed harmlessly beneath him.

FART SQUAD

Bertha's eyes bugged out in surprise. "Huh?"

Clutching his precious package, Harry darted toward a fire exit at the rear of the basement. Darren hesitated, torn between chasing after him and staying behind to help the Squad deal with B.O.

Could the rest of the Fart Squad take care of themselves?

Tina and Juan-Carlos faced off against Bertha and Oscar, who snickered at their seemingly unimpressive opponents.

"Seriously? A little girl and a clown?" Bertha jeered. "Is this a joke?"

Tina smiled slyly. "That depends," she said politely.

"On what?" Berta said, scowling.

"On who gets the last laugh."

Tina didn't seem to do anything but just stand there primly, but a powerful odor hit Bertha without warning. The looming bully toppled backward into the hole in the floor.

"One down," Tina said.

"Sis!" Oscar cried out, suddenly finding himself

outnumbered. He raised his sledgehammer nervously. "What did you do to her?"

Tina shrugged. "Who said I did anything?"

Oscar chickened out. He bolted for the stairs. "Get out of my way, you freaks!"

Juan-Carlos darted aside to let him pass, but, just as Oscar thought the way was clear, a stink bomb went off on the stairs, knocking him backward down the steps. He moaned at the foot of the stairs, all the fight banged out of him.

BLAP!

Darren grinned at Juan-Carlos. "Nice timing."

"I'm working on it," he said. "Now let's go get that Scratcher."

A voice from the ceiling called down to them.

"Aren't you forgetting something?" Walter said. "I wouldn't mind a little help getting down from here!"

Darren hesitated again. Harry was getting away. . . .

"Don't worry about Walter," Tina called out to Darren. "We'll help him out. You go after Harry."

"Yeah," Juan-Carlos chimed in. "Get that magic butt thingy back before we're all scratching ourselves like crazy!"

Darren trusted his squad to get Walter down from the ceiling.

Then he took off after Harry . . . and the Golden Scratcher!

CHAPTER TEN

Darren chased Harry out of the basement and up three flights of stairs. Huffing and puffing, Harry ran out onto the rooftop playground and slammed the door shut behind him. Darren grabbed the doorknob, but it refused to budge. A harsh odor seeped from the other side of the door. Darren recognized it right away.

Superglue! Couldn't Harry at least have come up with something new this time?

Harry had glued the lock shut, but that wasn't going to stop Darren. He turned around

and let loose with a volcanic *blatt* that melted the lock and blew down the door. Steam rose from the back of his trousers.

"Okay, that's more like it," he said, his butt still smarting from the eruption. "I had that one under control. Almost."

He rushed onto the roof just in time to see Harry pry open the lid of the wooden chest and reach inside for the Golden Scratcher. About a foot long, the gleaming instrument had curved metal claws at one end, all the better for scratching a persistent itch.

"Yes!" Harry gloated. "I can finally cure my itch!"

"Don't do it, Harry," Darren shouted. "I know about the curse, but it's too risky. You read the book. The Scratcher can't handle one more itch!"

"I don't care!" Harry snarled. "Stay out of this, Stonkadopolis. I told you before, this is

none of your business. Get lost!"

"Your buddies made it my business when they stole my lunch," Darren said.

"Those morons were supposed to take *all* the

lunches, so that everyone would eat those disgusting burritos, but then you and your nerdy buddy had to interfere so that I only got four measly lunches. *Everybody* was supposed to be farting like crazy, not just you and a few other kids. I wanted the whole school shut down!"

Darren stalled some more. "So then you tried again...."

"Yes! The next time the burritos were on the menu. And now the Scratcher belongs to me!"

Darren tried to reason with Harry.

"That was buried for a reason, remember? The

Scratcher can't take any more. If it blows, you could curse the whole town with itchy butts like yours!"

"So what?" Harry said. "It would serve everybody right for laughing at me all these years." He waved the Scratcher at Darren like a weapon. "Don't even try to talk me out of this. I've been waiting for this moment for too long!"

Before Darren could stop him, Harry reached around and put the Scratcher to use. A look of supreme relief came over his face.

"Oh my goodness!" he exclaimed. "It's working! It's killing the itch!"

Darren hoped that would be the end of it, but no such luck. After a few moments, an eerie glow lit up behind Harry, and the Scratcher started humming and throwing off sparks. Visibly frightened, Harry yanked the Scratcher away from his rear. More sparks flew.

"Uh-oh," he said sheepishly.

Darren resisted the temptation to say "I told you so."

The Golden Scratcher was glowing brighter and brighter, like a nuclear power plant running out of control. Darren could tell it was too late to bury it again. The Scratcher had reached its limit and was about to burst. Generations of Buttz itches were going to spill over the entire town—unless Darren could use his farts for good!

"Throw it away!" Darren shouted at Harry. "Hurry!"

Panicked, Harry hurled the sparking Scratcher away from him. It arced through the air.

"Watch out, Number Two!" Darren shouted.

"Don't call me that!"

Using every bit of energy in his gut, Darren blasted the flying Scratcher with a fiery ball of gas that completely incinerated it. All that was left was ashes—and a charred hole at the back of Darren's pants.

"Yikes!" Harry backed away, trembling.

The rest of the squad came rushing onto the roof. Darren half expected to see Bertha and Oscar chasing after them, but those two were nowhere in sight. "You take care of you-know-who?" he asked, pinching his nose to represent the smelly twins.

"Naturally," Juan-Carlos said. "Everyone knows that farts are stronger than B.O."

Tina looked around. "What happened to the Scratcher?"

"It's toast," Darren said. "Mission accomplished."

"Way to go, dude." Juan-Carlos high-fived him. "You're on fire. Get it?"

Tina groaned. "Yes, JC, we get it. We *always* get it."

Sirens blared below as police cars and fire engines converged on the school.

"Time to retreat!" Darren decided. He looked Walter over. "You think you can airlift all of us?"

"Absolutely." Walter fished a cold burrito from his pocket and stuffed his face. He swelled up like a hot-air balloon and started to lift off from the ground. Darren and Juan-Carlos grabbed his legs just in time. Tina scrambled onto his back and wrapped her tiny arms around his neck. "Hold on tight!" Walter said. "Prepare for takeoff!"

A tremendous fart blasted them all into the air. Walter zoomed off the roof, carrying the rest of the Squad with him. Within seconds, they were far away from Harry Buttz Elementary and the wailing fire engines. All of Buttzville stretched out below them.

"Yes!" Darren whooped. "We did it!"

Maybe this Fart Squad thing was going to be a lot of fun after all.

CHAPTER ELEVEN

Back at school, Stan took custody of the "special" burritos, saving them until the Fart Squad was needed again.

"Because that's the thing about farts," the janitor explained. "Just when you think you're all cleared out, an even bigger one comes along!"

With his farts finally under control, Darren found it easier to sit still in class. He even got a B on his report, which left out the part about the Buttz Curse and the Golden Butt Scratcher. Darren figured nobody would believe that part . . . and it would just upset Miss Priscilly's delicate sensibilities.

"A 'B' isn't bad," Andy assured him. "And every little bit of extra credit helps. You just need to find some way to burn off all that crazy energy of yours that doesn't involve getting into trouble."

"Actually," Darren said, "I think I know how to do that now."

"From great farts come mighty winds," Stan had said, and Darren believed him.

No matter the danger, the Fart Squad was ready to put the stink on the bad guys!

The End . . . for now.

Read a Sneak Peek of Book Two,
Fart Squad: Fartasaurus Rex

Out of nowhere, the tar pit bubbled and belched. It filled the air with a sour, stomach-turning smell that stank worse than a port-a-potty after a chili cook-off.

But the disgusting smell wasn't the worst thing rising from the pool of sticky black tar. Dozens of school kids on a field trip to the site stared wide-eyed at the pit. Their jaws dropped and their stomachs turned.

A gargantuan scaly head poked up from the gaseous soup. Prehistoric yellow eyes looked around at the modern world. Slimy drool dripped from hungry jaws. The tip of an enormous tail shot up from beneath the gooey surface of the pit. Bubbles burst from the tar, as if someone had let a giant fart rip in the bath, and a moment later, another nauseating burst of stink polluted the air, causing people to gag, plug their noses, and run for their lives.

FARTOSAURUS REX LIVED AGAIN!

CHAPTER ONE

EARLIER:

Darren Stonkadopolis had been looking forward to this field trip for weeks. As a die-hard dinosaur lover, Darren's favorite place to visit was the Buttzville Prehistoric Tar Pit & Museum. He never got tired of the local tourist attraction. Besides the pit itself, the museum contained fossils of ancient creatures trapped in the gooey tar millions of years ago, a museum, gift shop, and dinosaur-themed cafeteria. But the key piece of the museum's collection was the rarest of all dinosaurs, the long-extinct "Buttosaurus." It was the only one of its type and scientists believed it may have only ever existed in Buttzville.

"Check out those razor-sharp teeth," Darren said, pointing out to his best friend, Andy Blackman, as they admired the colossal skeleton, which towered above them on its hind legs outside the museum. Rows of sawlike fangs lined the dinosaur's bony jaws. "That's how you know it was a meat-eater. A predator!"

Andy probably already knew that, Darren figured. His friend was one of the brainiest kids at Buttzville Elementary School after all. But Darren couldn't resist raving about the skeleton and dinosaurs in general. They were just too cool to keep quiet about.

"Boy, wouldn't you like to see one of these in real life!"

Andy peered at the ferocious-looking skull through a thick pair of glasses. The tar had stained the bones a dark brown color. "Actually, I think I like keeping one hundred fifty million years between us."

While the entire fourth grade explored the paved pathways around the tar pit, the teacher in charge, Miss Priscilly, tried to keep all the children under control. She only had Stan, the school janitor, to help. He had also come along as an extra chaperone. The hardest kid to mind was also the richest—Harry Buttz Jr. The school and the town were named after his father. They still owned half of Buttzville. That's why Harry felt he could ignore the safety rail surrounding the pit and go in to get a closer look.

"Unhand me!" Harry squealed, when Stan grabbed him by the collar to save him from falling in. "I'll have your job!" he harrumphed as he tugged at his collar.

"Children, children!" Miss Priscilly called out. "Gather round and pay attention, while our host, Professor Paleo, kindly explains the educational value of this site."

The elderly museum curator had been conducting the tar pit tour ever since Darren was a little kid. He was a good friend of Darren's. Frizzy white hair escaped from under the pith helmet he wore. Professor Paleo winked at Darren before launching into his lecture, which Darren practically knew by heart:

"Millions of years ago, a prehistoric swamp existed where Buttzville now is. Liquid tar seeped up from the earth and created a deceptively deep pool. Dinosaurs and other primitive animals would wander over and some were unlucky enough to fall in it. Unlucky for them, but lucky for us. Their fossils were preserved in the pit when the tar hardened into thick, solid sludge. We've extracted many fossils from this site, such as that Buttosaurus skeleton on display over there. It is one of an entire genus of large-butted, vicious flesh-eating dinosaurs. Nobody knows how deep the pit goes, or what else might be trapped down there, preserved forever by the tar. . . ."